Not Quite a Story

A Collection of poems
by Philippa Tatham (1981-2015)

Not Quite a Story

A Collection of poems
by Philippa Tatham (1981-2015)

Foreword and commentary: Elizabeth Slinn
Editor: Marcus Whitfield
Photography: Ruth Anthony
Cover Art: Malcolm Brown

An introduction to Philippa

Philippa Margaret Tatham was born to me in Surrey on 15th September 1981. I later discovered that in the Catholic Church calendar, that day is the feast of Our Lady of Sorrows. There were just the two of us with my parents, Len and Noreen, in support on the side. Philippa was very close to them as they cared for her when I was at work. We stayed close by them and we all moved to Winchester in 1985 with my work, where she spent most of her growing years. Philippa thought everyone had a Mummy and a Mum and Dad, as she called us. That was one of life's shocks; when she went to school and discovered that not everyone's family model was like hers.

She was a grade A student all of her life. This high achieving tendency was typical of the personality type that develops anorexia, as she did twice in her life. She was 13 the first time and 23 the second, but her equal determination and stubbornness drove her through to some kind of survival each time.

Philippa showed great promise in her writing, indeed one of her primary school teachers predicted she might be a writer. Here is my first posthumous attempt at making that so.

She only wanted to be a writer or an actor; she came alive and hid from herself on the stage. She was a disciplined, committed and generous performer as she was in her friendships.

She went to Bristol to study Drama, refusing to apply for Oxbridge with her five A grade A levels. She achieved a first, of course. She went to London to find her way and was successful in the underground and amateur dramatic networks, but didn't find a break in the professional world and likewise with publishing of her work.

She had some very happy and joyful times full of friendships, hope and love. But she had the darkest of days as well, and we would all hold our breath wondering what she would do. After ten years of trying at life she contracted a painful skin condition that no one seemed to be able to treat. In the end, she gave up saying how she could have survived from 'passing happiness to passing happiness' but she couldn't see her way through the pain.
Here is some of her poetry, by which she lives on. It is carefully reproduced from her typewritten records, scraps of paper and a book. The punctuation is her own. As a precise practitioner of English grammar there is a

reason for her layout, which was all her own. The poems reflect her moods, her thoughts, her joys and dark spaces.

"I just want to be free", she wrote and now, made so by her own hand on 14th February 2015, she is. This warm and wilful, lovely and lively, intelligent and complex, friend, sister, niece, granddaughter and most beloved daughter of mine, Philippa.

- Elizabeth Slinn
January 2023

Some early poems, from 1999-2005, found in a handwritten book where she turned to the last page to write her final letter to us.

Homelessness (1999)

Cold.
You said.
It was so, so cold.
And in the warmth of a centrally heated house
I gazed into the heart of you
And saw you shiver.

I wanted to wrap you up
Enfold you in the hot water bottle heat of me
And bring you back, away
From the doorways and nightime and daytime
And drifting and wandering and cold of your memory.
I wanted to reach out.

I did it in my mind
Because I didn't know whether I should
Because I couldn't make a scene
Because I didn't know if you were quaking from the cold
Or retracting away from here, lost
In a house that wasn't you.

Drive me to Jerusalem (1999)

Philippa visited Jerusalem in 1994.

Drive me to Jerusalem
Drive me all the way
That I may drowse in grainy sun
And dream my life away.

Drive me to Jerusalem
I do not want to fly:
Slumped waiting in an airport
Hauling baggage through the sky.

Drive me to Jerusalem
For I have no pilgrim's staff:
I have no will to trudge the hills
No faith to hold my path.

Drive me to Jerusalem
And give me time to dream:
Let my eyes turn inwards
And ache upon the scene.

Drive me to Jerusalem,
But do not get me there,

For the Holy Town I touch in sleep
Is beyond compare.

Ghosts (1999)

We stood in the moon
In the blue, blue room
Sound hushed to breath
Streetlight to a fuzz.
I saw in the mirror a still, white spectre
Wiping, shifting
You, a long, soft shadow stretched
I felt you rise
And reach around me
True as frosted morning
Watched the warped pictures merging
I trembled as the last of me melted away
Quivered as I finally lost myself.
We curled, soundless, warm into each other.

You are my night time.
You are my hot, dark Hades.

Snowshaker sky (2001)

Bonfire smell
In our snowshaker world
Cold air bite
Burnt brown sky
In our snowshaker world.
Us looking out
Under the dome of the snowshaker sky
As dark earth hills
My face in your chest
Words no further than here
A moment of still
A moment of real
Before we are picked up, shaken up
And see us scuttle somewhere else.

From far away (2002)

Just thought I'd call-
Though I've nothing to say
 Except that I lack you.

Like a desert lacks the waters
Like a cut flower lacks the earth
Like a heart with a hole lacks.

I lack the smile you make me smile
The haze
Of a life in the sun
But most of all I lack the way you can make me feel like me.

Make me whole again
Turn me into an ocean
Let summer return.

Another Poem (2003)

It is colder
And older
On the other side of you.
I flew to the flame, but passion snuffed
Before we could suttee.
For a moment I melted
Away from dry leaves
Word-crammed
And in that tender second
It was a love
When the rest of the world was not
Before it caved in.
And now we are notches on bedposts
Another poem for my book.

Water Love (The Sponge) (2002)

You enter every pore of me
Worm in
Fill me up
Until I am heavy with you
Saturated and toppling
Once I was air, so light
I could dance atop you
Brush the surface
Barely touched
But you crept upwards, through me
Squeezed and drank me and now
I am drowning
Dragged down by your weight
Until I lie dying
Unseen
At the bottom of you.

Natural Choice (2002)

I cannot blame the stone
That I dash my own self against
For hurting.
If I sink into an ice- cream
I cannot berate it
For making my teeth scream
No matter how the tears fall as I keep licking.

But the cuckoo-
The cuckoo as she perches on the rock
Delicate as flower, and cracks it-
The cuckoo, who renders even my downy nest
Barren and
Hostile.
She who wins-
She can stab me with a thousand pins
As I tumble into my own stupidity.

Survivor (2004)

I have broken the surface
And am gasping and glugging,
Struggling to breathe.
This is the worst
The swim to shore
Treading water
Kicking the stone tied to your feet
That still calls you down
To silent, searing
Void.
How wonderful the light glimpsed from below!
Gold, the abyss becomes worthwhile
As we dream upwards.
How vicious and cruel the cold air
When you get there.

I want to live
But I cannot scream here
Without being heard
Disturbed
I am not filled, embraced,
And though it was death caressed me
At least I was held, kept
Cavernous world without will not

Unify, unite
But ignores me completely
A tiny squiggle
Unsure how to do
Just trying to stay afloat
Not panicking
At least in drowning, you know where you are.

Ode to Mushrooms (2004)

The silliest drug, it seems to me
Is psychedelic LSD.
Take heroine, or crack or coke
And all those things you sniff or smoke-
Provided that it's decent stuff
And not like many dealers, rough-
On their effects you may rely
They calm you down or make you high
But there is no such guarantee
With zany things like LSD.
And though hallucinogenic tripping
Often will appear quite ripping
Other days it's not so great
And land you in a sorry state
And though I know primeval savages
Use it in their rite of passages
It may inflict untold ravages
Or simply have you plucking cabbages
From thin air; you just don't know
Which way the drug is going to go.
Take young Peter for example
Who only tried a tiny sample
And at once before him saw
Iguanas crawling out the floor.

Poor Peterkins was terrified
And ran into the woods to hide
And nevermore, since that sad hour
Has he been seen,'cept picking flowers
In the forest, some perceive
An unkempt figure 'mongst the trees.
Or note the case of my friend Claire
Who spent a week-end as a chair.
For two whole days, without improving
She sat rigid and unmoving-
(Although I must right now confer
My thanks, for it is down to her
That at my last, much praised soiree
-a small and intimate party-
Though one chair short I was still able
To seat all guests around the table).
So if you really want the best
From drugged experience, I suggest
You follow this one simple tenet,
Keep clear of all hallucinogenics.
Stay faithful to your marijuana
And you'll live happily ever after.

Mothers Day (2005)

This is about my father Len. Philippa and he had a special accord. She had burnt the pudding and ran away to the allotments. He went and found her.

My body was an earthquake
Screaming with grief
And Monstrous I hid
Too vile to be in the company
To belong at the table
In the band
Of Love.

And so, you see, I ran away
Crouched like
The lumpen beast I am
In the cold concrete ditch and filled it with
Dry sobs
Tears
And snot.

But you came

Warm bones stretched
To search for me
And with a touch that told
Of the love inside your wise old eyes
And a voice that spoke
Of care that I will never bequeath
You held my hand
And brought me home.

Later poems, 2005 to 2015

These poems were found on a USB memory stick which she told us about in her note.

Bed

Oh Bed you are amazing
Oh Bed you are the best
When I sink beneath your covers
I know that I am blessed
Oh Bed you a wonder
Oh Bed you are so fly
You're better than a puppy
You're better than a pie
A desk just doesn't cut it
And neither does a chair
I've slept on bus and taxi
But they simply can't compare
Oh Bed we should be married
Oh Bed please say 'I do'
And I swear no more to spend
Another day
Away
From
You

The Song of the Arts Student

This was probably written with great feeling as she had to work as a receptionist to pay the rent.

I got all As in my exams
Got a first class degree
And so at work, you know, I am
The best at making tea.
They always said that I'd go far
That my analyses
On Freud and Plato were gold star
But now I make the tea
I'm good at coffee too, and cake
I file and type quite finely
I fill the printers, and I make
The boardroom tea sublimely
I screen all calls and order flowers
I smile and book your travel
I stare at Facebook hours on hours
And let my mind unravel
I listen to your pains and woes
Arrange your birthday supper

I buy your gifts, dry clean your clothes
Then brew you up a cuppa
I once read Milton, Keats and Joyce
Once wept at Shakespeare's sonnets
I studied war, peace, Hobson's choice
And eighteenth cent'ry bonnets
I marked the death cries at Cullodden
Used words non-ironically
Like 'ribald,' 'infer' and 'postmodern'
So that's now how I make tea.
For I have grown up, and away,
From such tomfoolery
And the cleverest thing you'll hear me say
Is 'How'd you like your tea?'
For Chomsky does not pay too well
De Beauvoir is a pauper
So it's better not, when skint, to dwell
On Sartre, Pope or Chaucer
For pens are bought on broken dreams
And toilets cleaned with hoping
And once ambition's burst its seams
You cannot keep on moping.
To earn half-decent wages, you
Must smarten up, like me
And leave your books, they'll never do
And learn to make good tea.

Fission

As with all of her poems her punctuation is reproduced as she wrote, undoubtedly with purpose.

Mother you are my nuclear origin
In you I was forged, in your roar transformed, then
Heaving you sputtered me forth.
Still you broil
More than a burning.
Your heat sears the atom
Fuses
And creates life,
Your glare is outrageous
A brilliance scorching at a billion miles, and across the light years I call you
I the spark a flicker on earth.
I bask open hearted in your distant existence, at
A love so enraged that it shoots through the vacuum and rains down
Upon me. And in it I unfurl, grow roots.
In this foreign soil I am divine fire

A beanstalk stretching to heaven
I am your votary, the sunlover, sun flower
In this system not yours I am your credit.
But should you draw me back –
For your gravity is a stone upon my chest ,
A black hole of sheer mass,
Mother dear, I will collapse
And evaporate.

Love

Before he was a boy, Love was a force
That drew the moon to Earth
And earth to Sun
It divided and pulled together
Shaped a cosmos
A heart flicker
It made chains and wanting
Attracting repelling
Hatred at the poles
And order from nonsense grew and quelled
Its own womb and made it a son
A boy it could control
A drive outside the living soul,
But no thing wants to be alone
Even the atom seeks to give, to take, to make
Itself a bond and something more, a planet perhaps,
A strand of DNA.
Eros fragmented inhabits us still.

Grass

The rage in a blade of grass when the wind blows
Is unendurable.
It bends, one in a million, all the same
Observing its cousin
An oak
Stand firm and crack
Root ripped
The last stance a spectacle
But futile nonetheless
Still dead in the end
And the mountain ground inexorable
To broken bits of gravel
And Babels of glass sway till they shatter in the mad air's clinch
Yes, grass understands it is better
To bow,
Remain irrelevant and meek
To give way to God when he puffs out his cheeks
Let him pass without trial
Let him do as he pleases and watch him go
But even so
Lying face to feet

Even a lawn swears vengeance.

For J, on the riverbank

Teenage years were spent around the Itchen navigation way.

A walk in mud, and the flood
Of memories bobbing helpless in weeds
And lulling us back to silt-soft hours
Like hands reaching for a child
On the rickety bridge
When I jumped for a ball, stripped for a man
Leaped for a thrill
Into hidden rock beneath the frond-life.
When you made love on the hill above
And I in the dark below.

Looking through a thistle I watch the world
The church and the stream
Wound
Around meadows like a loved one's hair
And the glare of a future now forgot, washed pale
In a breeze as sweet as we were
Once.

The graffiti in the ironwork will not wear
Sheltered from the rain and air,
In girders etched
By school folk
Our folk
Boys and girls a-screaming for a screw, you
Laugh
I do too
At a puberty that never stops.

Berries without worms peer through hedges
Offering a nibble
A token of the times
I pass by someone
I once knew.
But the green and the breeze fade us away
Till it cannot matter anyway
That my old heart
Keeps beating.

Unshriven

See me tie myself in knots,
In bows and ribbons of spider legs
Of a rosary rotted
Of my tender fingers wrenched
Bent
For the good of you -
And for me too,
I suppose
I guess.

See me peg
My hands to the cross,
And bind them together, chain them to a rock
So I might not
In a slip of unthinking
Stretch toward you,
Touch you
Much
Where others can see –
And observe too the cleft
Of a tongue split in two, so forked I
Utter only these blessed untruths
Of not knowing

Or wanting
Or holding you.

See,
I keep the peace,
Put a stitch in my lips,
Nothing released from between the blades
Of my fast clenched teeth,
And yea, lest even now I fall to you
And confess
Lest I
Mistakenly relate
A passion unreciprocate
A need uninvited
Then see in my skins
In those many threads shed by
Shed for
You,
See in these,
In me,
The weals of a hessian penitence
And
Hexed,
Thricely feel
How my hidden
Unspoken

And unforgiven deeds turn back
And gnaw me inside out.

A Summertime in Britain

A summertime in Britain
Is rarely ever hot
And in Frimley, Frome and Fritton
It will rain as like as not
In Brighton, sun might glimmer
For a day, in Bournemouth, two
But too sun the sky grows dimmer
And the clouds block out the view
No, a summertime in Britain
Is really not much fun
And I'm not remotely smitten
By its intermittent sun
But you, you're bright and lovely
And you never let me down
And the sun shines bright above me
Whenever you roll into town.
When I'm a famous poet
I will write your name in stars
Then the universe will know it
From Macclesfield to Mars
And our love will last eternal
Come summer, hail or snow
And in the pages of my journal

You and I will always glow.

The Smile

It is a static smile
In the centre of my brain,
You fur at the edges, withdraw
And though I search, yet no more
Of this story will happen, will occur
To me.
I remember a night
A hand held bent across your chest
As you slept like angel, like a devil, like a man who knew
And did what he was made to do,
And at that moment in the still
In the strange chilled hours of a fetid want
Exploded
Gratified
Fulfilled,
I stroked you, loved you
The way a creature standing outside time
Can love the one beside her
The one who dreams
And smiles
And clings contented
Devoted

For that split
Atoms breadth
Yes you are a picture
A word encased and separate,
You are a phrase that breeds no more but this
Itself,
And in that smile there lies
Tangled,
Confused
Perfection.
Yes, in that smile
The tale ends
And we are finished
Nothing but a past
Complete.

Just Another Notch

I knew from the start
That love was a thing too huge to ask
From someone as sweet
And as cruel as you.
Yes I knew,
So I never expected
Though I hoped
That you might
That I might
Rest,
As safe in your words
As I was in your arms,
Yes, I hoped,
But rarely believed
Or let myself dwell
On the thought
For a moment
That you would
That you could
Relinquish the comfort
Of a nice girl's bed
Cast off her love
Take the risk that was me;
And though I could see all along

That truth inside your sea changed,
Innocent eyes,
That you'd never be strong enough
Brave enough
To hold me through my mutations
To grip me as I writhed;
Though I never expected that you'd survive
This first trial of fidelity
Yet it doesn't sting less
Prick me less
That I was right.

Beautiful Suicide

It was a beautiful suicide
Lost in those leaves of hot chocolate
An immersion in divinity, as if
A drink could be an art
Geometrics in a cup,
As if it longed to tell a truth
Where my spoon dipped in.

A beautiful death at a scrubbed wood board
While the trains clumped above, overriding the thoughts
That stuck, appalled
In a gullet too dry for talking
Till I breathed
And swallowed
Wished to dissolve in your great green
Sea clean eyes
In the face that never grows old
But sipping your tea I mustered round
And fuel to your good
To my fear,
I said we were no more.
What precious ghosts we were,
As night crossed the river and the rain fell down

And the city crooned about us,
Purple in the wink of a million lights
As life continued and a man with no shoes
Buried his head
Begged
In silence for a penny
And we passed on, treading the bridge as soft as skin
And the sound of some cello
Dreamed of a sadness
A dance never been
And we kissed and I touched you
One more time
And we said our goodbyes
Then you fled into the dark
And I hid in the arches
And cried.

Bookcase

I want to be your bookcase
I want to wind around the wood
Inside the leaves you read
I want to learn you in those fantasies opened up
And wandered through
I want my cheek and spine to lie here in your hands
I want the hard thoughts of you
I want to watch you, come to you through pine scent and tree pulp
And ink,
And be picked
Bit by bit
By you.
I want to be the lamp that stands above you
Unlit
I want to stay upright at midnight while you lie asleep
I want to watch your back glow smooth as moon
I want to see your hair fall like spiderwebs across you
And sweet dreams drift
In the pits of your brain
I want to be the pipe you suck

I want the smoke you draw to soothe you
Satisfy
I want you to play me as you play the tubes
Fingers flying
I want to bubble and gasp as you drag at me
I want to be the shot of fire imbibed
Swilled, relished, judged, desired
I want to be your taste
Acquired
I want to be the pliers
The hammer, the level and nails
I want to be your tools entire
Taken forth to clip a wire, turn a screw
Knuckles clenched on me, firm in your grip
I want to be used by you
To fix
And I want to be your necklace
To gleam black and green
And dandle down your warm white skin
I want to rest against you, move as you move, you
Fascinate me,
Hold me
Until I want to be me
With you
Wrapped in tenderness more true

Than today or tomorrow or Happy Evermore
Than how it was before
I want to be the moth wings
Uncrushed that we flutter upon
And I want to be now,
Just now
That's all.

The Sewing Group
Or
Fates Remastered

She persuaded the group to give her membership as a kind of writer in residence!

They knit and sew and stitch and knot
They tat and drink and natter
They talk for hours on God knows what
But who cares? It doesn't matter.
They patch and darn demented dreams
Weave words as deft as spiders
They split opinions at the seams
Then drink a few more ciders
They stretch out thoughts on looms of wine
Thread pasts through skeins of present
Arrange new futures neat in line
Speak truths more right than pleasant
So souls are spun and visions wrung
And worlds are made of cotton
And wool gets wound and songs get sung
With half the words forgotten

And universes rise and fall
As needles crack and rattle
And hats and scarfs march, great and small
Like empires off to battle
They chant and mutter through their beer
Their gossip flows unending
Some may call them quaint, or jeer
The socks and hearts they're mending
But though they can seem odd or kitsch
They'd best not hear your laughter
For one quick snip, a single stitch
And it's the end of ever after.

Sonnet 30

Sometimes my poor old soul requires
A good old fashioned blubber
To brood on aged and past desires
Erased by Death's great rubber
Sometimes I need a quiet spot
To weep quite unimpeded
To dwell upon the barren lot
My genius, still unheeded.
Sometimes I have to mourn my luck
My friends all lost and withered
And how, in short my life doth suck
When all things are considered
I need to brood on old regrets
My future full of new ones
My noble deeds that fate forgets
And how I'm frankly sue one.
But when I've cried out every fear
Re-lived each pain and muddle
The best thing is that you're still here
With a cuppa and a cuddle.

Iceland

She had a wonderful, romantic holiday here in 2012.

I'll tell you a tale
Of snow.
Four feet deep with splintered toes
And thirteen bad boys running through the blue
The pink
Thirteen murderers spinning where lights arch and sink
And swirl in a kiss
And an old woman tramps with her sack on her back
And ponies walk each other's footsteps
Where we walk each other's footsteps
Sparkling hard past the fields and the farms
Yes, I'll tell you a tale of
Glittering sticks to gird a road
And snow that blows in hurricanes and batters the bear
The white bear
We hide inside
While the ponies turn their eyes, stubbornly enduring

To the sun.
I'll tell you a tale of a plough dyed green by a dancing night
And the plough we trail behind
Blind,
Of the white that glints and a warm inside
A crack in a bed where we lie
Side by side
In our home
A stove blushing red like a virgin bride
Or a wife who left her gown outside
In the white
And the talk over dinner, the hands held and kisses held
For photographs
And sometimes just because.
I'll tell you of water, frozen
Where it falls
Of the churn and the guern and the gods in the ice
Statues beyond human
Statues like humans
Fangs of the rockface
Twisting in a single, agonised
Bliss
Till spring.

I'll sing of the Christmas bird torn through a wheel
And the backwards down a mountainside
And the winds
That laugh as we howl and roar
On bright white wastes and
An eruption below, waiting for the moment
The instant
To blow.
I sing of the fox unseen
The man
And the machine
I sing,
I sing
A graveyard, a parliament
Lazuli pennies and pools
Where maidens
Unmaidened
Died
And where water so clear it could sing
Sings for a hand
An offering.
I sing
I sing
I'll tell you a tale

Of two worlds, two plates, a line where they collide
And lie unstill, like the restless dead
I sing of mud boiled until it bursts and
Black stone and iron waves and
A woman who sailed off the edge of the earth
And returned.
I sing I sing
I tell you a tale
Of snow and a church and a steaming heat
Where the sun glows low and we touch evermore
And where tunnels trundle like the seats
The holes
Of gnomes
Of trolls
And where
There in the silence
There, there in the silence
Yes there in the silence
A heart
Still
Beats.

The Tube

Her daily endurance on the Northern Line.

The tube pulls up, the tube pulls out
A door won't shut so people shout
A coat's got trapped, a bag is caught
Folk stretch for the bars, but they're all too short
A tall man stoops to the shape of the wall
A heel snaps, a lady falls
An old man's crushed in the rush and the heat
And frowns at a woman who offers her seat
Baby on board says a woolly lapel
Opening space with its Sesame spell.
Shuffle and bustle, Move down, move on up
The tension and sweat overfloweth the cup
A hand on a thigh, a chin on a chest
Stranger on stranger likes fossils are pressed
Like fossils
Like Limestone
Like fish in a tin
Turning to rock as they squeeze themselves in
A man with a rucksack, a man with a beard
A man with a can and with eyes that look weird
A protest, a zealot, a beggar, a sign

A suicide jumped and shut down the whole line
But we cannot be late and we cannot turn back
We've got meetings and deadlines and dates to attack
We've got lovers a-waiting , an ex spouse or two
We've got mortgages, migraines and stones in our shoe
An i-pod on full and a Kindle on glare
Free newspapers tuck to the chewing-gummed chair
Churning and grunting the tube chunders on
Everyone's winning but no body's won
Nobody's won though we've suits Saville-made
Though we've leopardskin boots and a shirt in red plaid
Though we're dressed to impress, though we're ready to fly
Thought we've energy, balls and a mental high-five
Still, the tube chunders through us, the tube trundles past
And the doors still come down on my Burberry scarf
And the whistles still blow and the loudspeakers blare

And the pregnant and old still wage war for a chair
And the lovers still wait and the meetings still meet
And the tourists still dawdle and clog up the street
But the brakes rattle on and the metal still screams
And we still join the press in this city of dreams.

Cardinal's Cap

She wears her red like a cardinal's cap
Like a queen in the teeth of the turning year,
She wears her red like a bleeding sun,
Streaking the leaves as gold as hair
As honey
As brown as the earth that she perches upon
Until stained a shade of blackthorn briars,
Of fox tail
They curl in the fires of her smoke swilled eyes
Crisp and drop
And bob with the acorns through stainless skies
And streams
While she,
She speaks too much
Twitters too much
Tells tales that too often are better untold
Weaving her prattle through a bone-sharp cold
Through air that gnaws like a maggot or a deer
A hunger that burrowed in her seared skin
Seeks shelter,
As a spear might hide awhile in a side
And pushes away from the punctured thought
Yes she wears her red like the Wise,

Like the well-sought
Like the sacrifice of lamb-locks
To knowing, for the prize
Of a time when the winds will wind
Tight
Around her
Just as the dying, the soft sighing days
Have sworn they could,
For she wears her red
Like the newly born,
Like the unfledged and already torn
She wears her red like a berry, as ripe
As winter, as a field of corn
And alone, unmourned
Unmissed
She will talk,
Will chatter unsatisfied
To the bored abyss
Wishing, yes wishing that she might catch
Some small word, some answer back
A momentary recompense for that
Still undisclosed
Openness,
For that tear yet redder
Than a cardinal's cap..

We Danced

We danced
I don't know what to
We had done it before
For seconds at a time
Though you didn't
Nor would
As a rule
You sat
And smoked
And watched
As a rule
But in that room atop the rain and the streets
Steeped in a heat, in a haze that blotted us awhile
Safe and away from the white city eyes
We were drunk
And alone
And happy
And as some sound struck up from somewhere
Your arms fell around me
Your body fell around me
And we flickered, sunk between who we were
And are

And though we don't
Though we never
Still our hands pressed together in the old
fashioned way
My head leant against you in that age old play
Of being
And though we don't
Though we aren't
Yet in that moment
Still
We danced.

If you walk away from me

If you stand ashamed
If you never speak again to me
And pretend I've gone astray
Or maybe never was
If you forget how I felt, how I smelt
If how I twined and tossed and talked and breathed
Gets lost
Somewhere
If you omit
The matter of my speech
A chatter unstinting, that wincing
You kissed and overspoke
And melted into something better
If you forget the long, wet
Line of tongue you drew across
And inside me,
The cries you gleaned
For you
From me
If my sighs flee relieved from memory,
Then please be aware
That while sad
And unfair

Yet I know and I welcome this innocent pain
The burnings that break me over again
And though I might falter
Yet still I shan't care
For in lighting your matches
And swimming in your flames
I knew there would be
A sting to retain
And though the wounds whimper
As we weary the game
 I can still burst the window
And look up to the rain
And though I may bore you
And we both itch for change
I can still run out singing
And dance in the rain.

I want to drive a tractor

One of her children's poems

I want to drive a tractor
I want to drive a train
I want to be an actor
And to fly an aeroplane
I want to see Atlantis
And to pet a dinosaur
I want a praying mantis
And to roar like lions roar
I want to feed the sparrows
I want to swim to France
And grow prize winning marrows
And to head a conga dance
My mum says that I'm foolish
And I ought to settle down
That I ought to be more schoolish
And stop acting like a clown.
She says I need to focus
And to be more realistic
But I want hocus pocus
And some magic party biscuits.
I want to wake up singing
I want to get all As

And to hear the town bells ringing
Through the lazy summer days
I want a snowy Christmas
And to build a lunar station
And get clever words like 'isthmus'
Into normal conversation
My mum says I'm a dreamer
That life's doomed to disappoint
That my mind would be serener
If I stopped trying to stand on point
She says I cannot take it
That for us, fame will not be
But hey, someone has to make it
And it may as well be me.
And so I'll dream adventures
And I won't give up on fun
And then when I'm old with dentures
I'll look back at what I've done
And I'll laugh and cheer and chirrup
Forget all my woes and pains
Then put my foot back in the stirrup
And I'll do it all again.

One of many ditties

Silly stupid foolish me
For ever thinking we could be
Any more than one more song
About a love that went all wrong.

Graveyard

When I am in the Garden of Remembrance where some of her ashes are with her Grandfather's and now joined by her Grandmother's, I look at the tree and repeat this poem, resting in the shade that is hers.

In a darkness like this
A thickness like this
There is rest.
When the soil bungs your ears and lungs
And lids droop in the pressure of six feet down,
When flowers wind shyly, roots probing for entry,
Lapping at the juice that was you and
Turning it to petals, leaves, briars, fruit,
Becoming the lover that knows you from the organs out
That transforms density to blue
And pink and green
When you are the shade you drowse beneath and dream,

Then, then there is sleep
And peace
And something perhaps near contentedness.

Printed in Great Britain
by Amazon